Forever...

Emma Dodd

When you're happy, full of fun,
I will be happy too.

And when you giggle, laugh and run,
I'll laugh along with you.

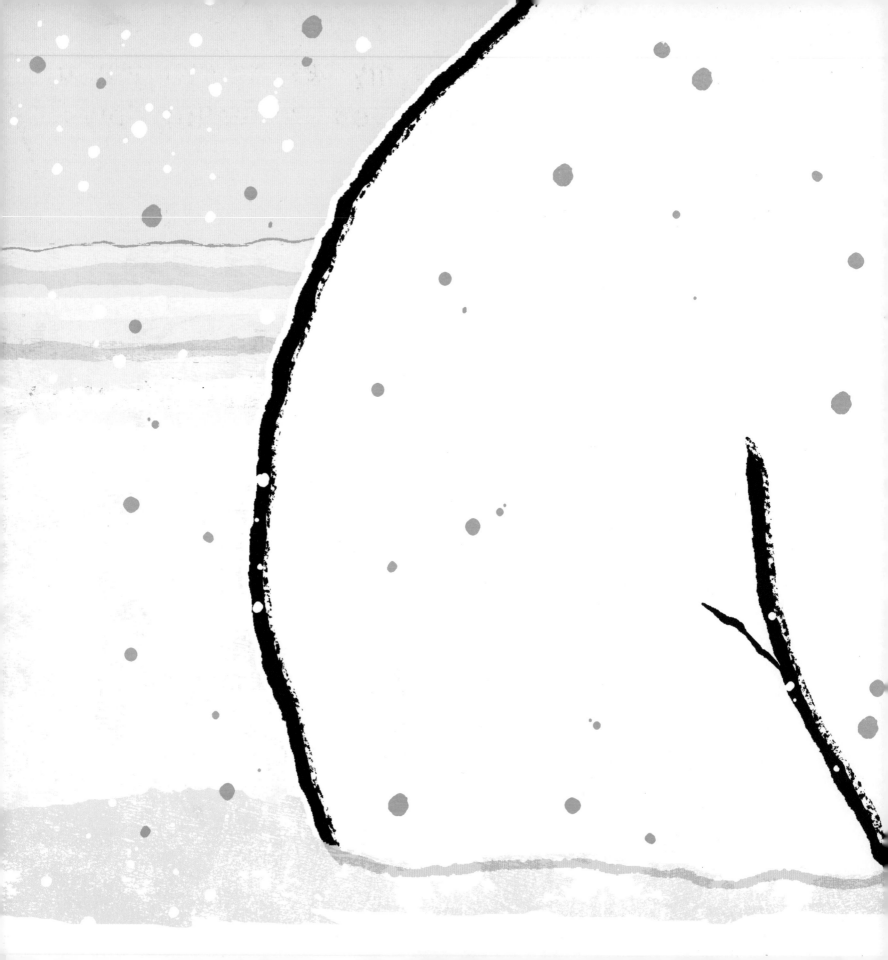

I'll do my best to pick you up
when you are feeling down.

I'll try to find your lovely smile
and smooth away your frown.

When you're scared and feel unsure,
you'll find me right beside you.

If you're ever feeling lost,
you know I'll always find you.

When you share your
hopes and plans,
I'll keep them safe for you.

I promise I'll do all I can
to make your dreams come true.

And as through all the years to come
we journey on together,

deep within my heart,
I know
I will love you...

forever.

A TEMPLAR BOOK

First published in the UK in 2013 by Templar Publishing
This softback edition published in 2014 by Templar Publishing,
an imprint of The Templar Company Limited,
Deepdene Lodge, Deepdene Avenue, Dorking, Surrey, RH5 4AT
www.templarco.co.uk

1 3 5 7 9 10 8 6 4 2

ISBN: 978-1-84877-174-1

Printed in China